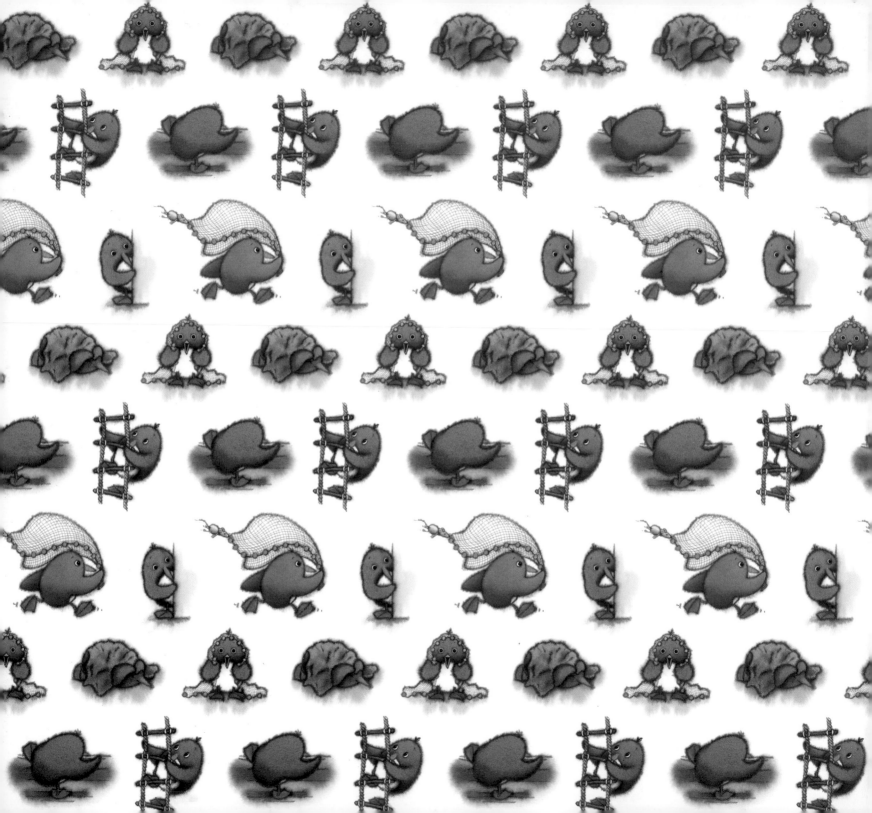

Books by Marcus Pfister

THE CHRISTMAS STAR*
DAZZLE THE DINOSAUR*
HANG ON, HOPPER!
HOPPER*
HOPPER HUNTS FOR SPRING*
HOPPER'S EASTER SURPRISE
HOPPER'S TREETOP ADVENTURE
I SEE THE MOON
MILO AND THE MAGICAL STONES*

PENGUIN PETE*
PENGUIN PETE AND LITTLE TIM
PENGUIN PETE AND PAT*
PENGUIN PETE'S NEW FRIENDS*
PENGUIN PETE, AHOY!*
THE RAINBOW FISH*
RAINBOW FISH TO THE RESCUE!*
SHAGGY
WAKE UP, SANTA CLAUS!

*also available in Spanish

For Nina Catharina

Copyright © 1993 by Nord-Süd Verlag AG, Gossau Zürich, Switzerland
First published in Switzerland under the title *Pit ahoi!*
English translation copyright © 1993 by North-South Books Inc.

First published in the United States, Great Britain, Canada,
Australia, and New Zealand in 1993 by North-South Books,
an imprint of Nord-Süd Verlag AG, Gossau Zürich, Switzerland.
First paperback edition published in 1998.

Library of Congress Cataloging-in-Publication Data
Pfister, Marcus.
[Pit ahoi! English]
Penguin Pete, ahoy! / by Marcus Pfister ; translated by Rosemary Lanning.
Summary: Penguin Pete befriends Horatio, a mouse dwelling on a shipwreck,
and finds that he has a lot to learn about life on board a ship.
[1. Penguins—Fiction. 2. Mice—Fiction. 3. Ships—Fiction.] I. Title.
PZ7.P448559Pj 1993 [E]—dc-20 93-19921

A CIP catalogue record for this book is available from The British Library.
ISBN 1-55858-220-7 (trade binding)
3 5 7 9 TB 10 8 6 4
ISBN 1-55858-221-5 (library binding)
1 3 5 7 9 LB 10 8 6 4 2
ISBN 1-55858-907-4 (paperback)
3 5 7 9 PB 10 8 6 4
Printed in Belgium

For more information about our books, and the authors and artists
who create them, visit our web site: www.northsouth.com

# Penguin Pete, Ahoy!

By Marcus Pfister

TRANSLATED BY ROSEMARY LANNING

North-South Books / New York

Penguin Pete woke up one bright, sunny morning and said to himself, "This feels like a good day to go exploring." He plunged straight into the sea and swam quickly past all the friendly fish. "Sorry, no time to play today," he said. "I've got important things to do."

Before long Pete found something really interesting to explore. Around the bend in the next bay was an old ship with jagged holes in its rotten timbers and tattered sails flapping in the wind.

There seemed to be no one on the ship, so Pete clambered on board.

"What a mess!" gasped Pete, looking at all the crates, barrels, ropes, and broken planks scattered across the deck. A sudden rustling noise startled him. It seemed to come from under an old sack. Pete waddled quietly over to the sack and pulled it into the air.

Cowering underneath was a little grey mouse.

"Hello," said Pete. "I'm sorry if I frightened you, but I was a bit scared myself. I didn't think there was anyone on this ship."

"There's only me," said the little creature. "And I wasn't really frightened." The mouse stood up straight and saluted smartly. "I'm Horatio, the ship's mouse," he announced. "Welcome aboard!"

"Nice to meet you, Horatio. I'm Penguin Pete. Let's be friends."

"All right," said Horatio. "Come on, I'll show you my ship."

Pete liked the storeroom best of all. Some of the boxes and packages were broken open, and Pete had never seen so many good things to eat.

"Does all of this really belong to you?" asked Pete, licking his beak.

"It certainly does," said Horatio with pride. "Help yourself!"

"Let's go back on deck," said Pete when he was too full to eat any more.

Pete rushed upstairs and found a fishing net to play with. He swished it through the air, used it to give his friend a ride, even dressed up in it . . . until suddenly he was tangled in the mesh. The more he struggled to get free, the more entangled he became.

"Don't worry!" said Horatio. "A ship's mouse can handle nets. I'll get you out of there."

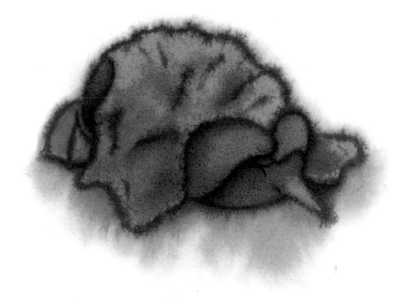

Next Horatio suggested a game of hide-and-seek. Pete tried his best, but he wasn't very good at hiding, and the mouse, who knew every nook and cranny on the ship, quickly found him every time.

"Let's climb to the top of the mast," said the mouse. "You can see the whole world from up there."

He scampered nimbly up the rope ladder. Pete struggled to follow him.

"The view from here is wonderful, isn't it?" said Horatio.

"Yes," said Pete. "But I don't like being so high up. I'm feeling dizzy."

"You're just seasick," said Horatio wisely.

"I think I'd feel better in the sea," said Pete. "Why don't we go for a swim?"

"Swim?" said the little mouse nervously. "I have a better idea. I'll ride in the lifeboat. It still looks seaworthy. You can push me."

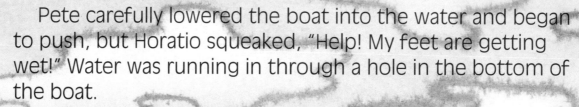

Pete carefully lowered the boat into the water and began to push, but Horatio squeaked, "Help! My feet are getting wet!" Water was running in through a hole in the bottom of the boat.

"Abandon ship!" called Pete.

"But I can't swim!" cried the little mouse.

"I'll save you!" shouted Pete as he raced to pull Horatio out before the boat sank.

"Climb on my back," said Pete. "You'll be all right."

He carried his little friend back to the ship and wrapped him in a blanket. The mouse was still trembling with fright.

"I think I'll stay on the ship from now on," he said. "But I hope you'll come to visit me again."

"Of course I will," said Pete as he jumped into the sea.

Horatio scurried to the ship's rail to wave good-bye. "Ahoy there, Pete!" he called.

"So long, shipmate!" cried Pete as he paddled away. "The next time I come to visit I'll teach you how to swim!"

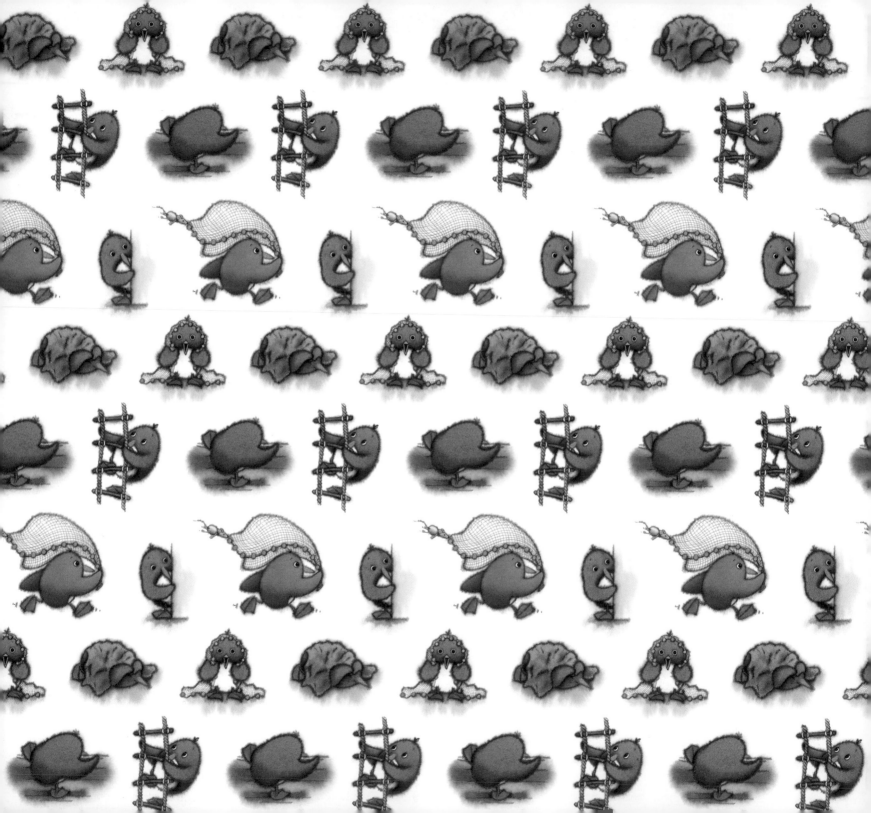

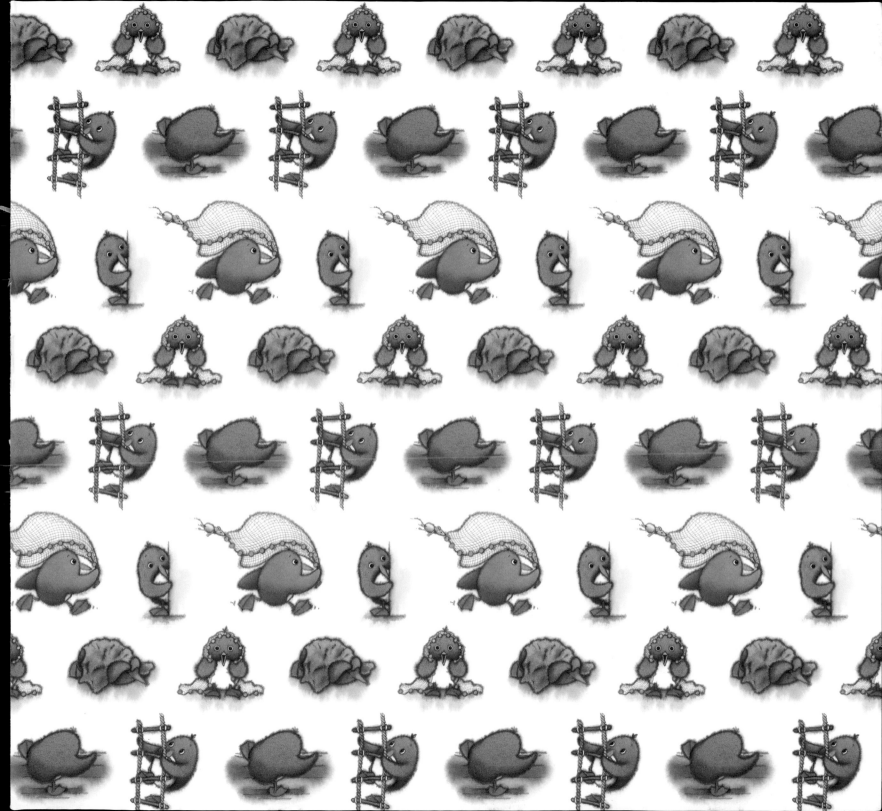